THE CONCRETE GARDEN

BOB GRAHAM

WALKER BOOKS
AND SUBSIDIARIES
LONDON • BOSTON • SYDNEY • AUCKLAND

After a cold, hard winter,
doors opened.

G

Fifteenth floor.
Going down.
Amanda took the
box from her mum.

Ground floor.

For the Smart Street kids.
Written in the time of Covid.

Thanks to Rose and Oli and
their kitchen table drawings.

First published 2023 by Walker Books Ltd, 87 Vauxhall Walk, London SE11 5HJ • © 2023 Blackbird Design Pty Ltd • The right of Bob Graham to be identified as author of this work has been asserted in accordance with the Copyright, Designs and Patents Act 1988 • Printed in China • All rights reserved. No part of this book may be reproduced, transmitted or stored in an information retrieval system in any form or by any means, graphic, electronic or mechanical, including photocopying, taping and recording, without prior written permission from the publisher. • British Library Cataloguing in Publication Data: a catalogue record for this book is available from the British Library • ISBN 978-1-5295-1264-9 • www.walker.co.uk • 10 9 8 7 6 5 4 3 2

Children spilled out
like sweets from a box.

Amanda was last out.

She brought chalks.
First she chose green.

All in all, Amanda was quite
pleased with her work.

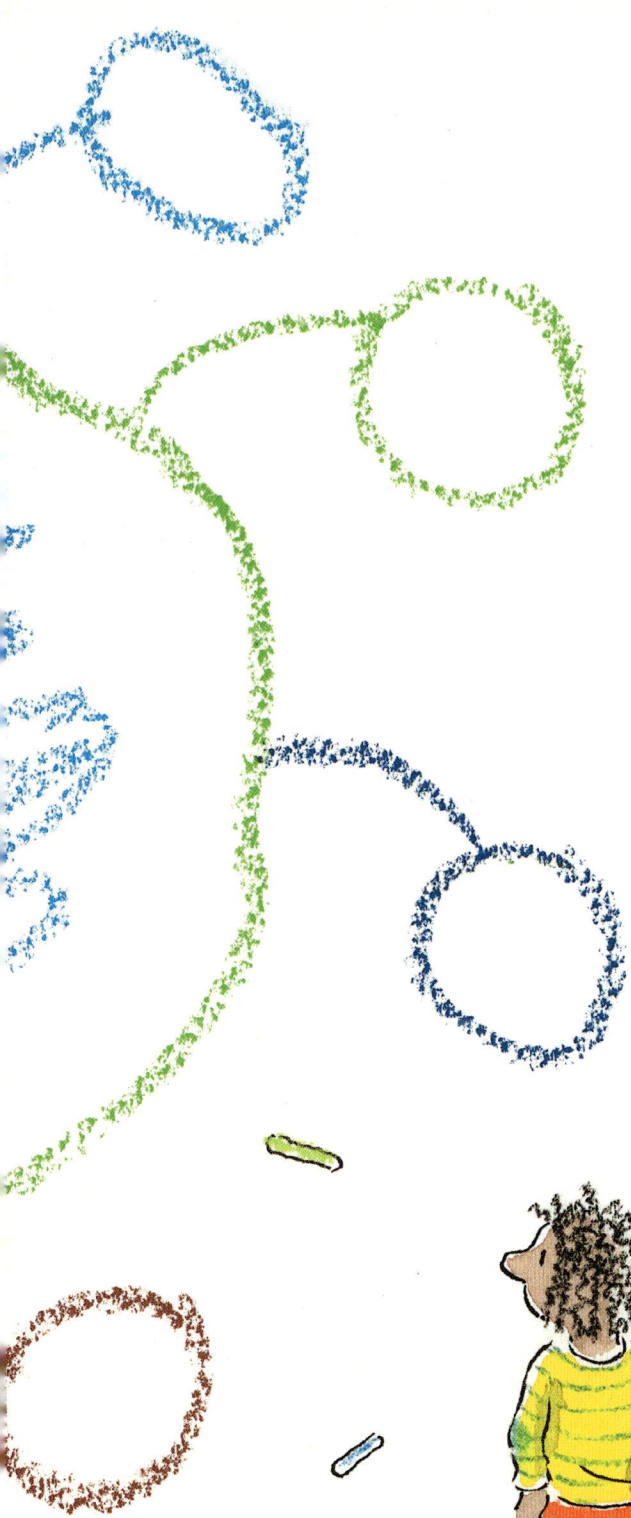

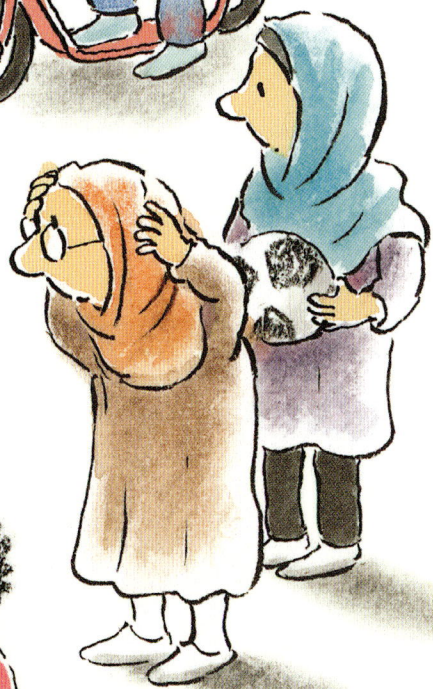

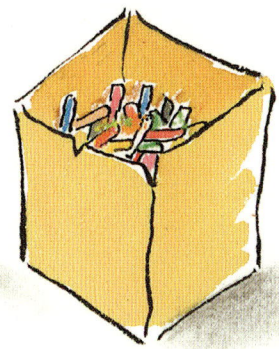

Then Jackson made
a dandelion out of it.
Simple as that!

Janet Fairly worked hard on a mushroom.
The Bradley twins added flowers.

As a brief and silent scuffle
emerged between two toddlers,
Lovejoy put a very large snail
on the mushroom.

It was Luke's dog Alfie
who smudged the
Bradleys' flowers.

And it was Indira who saw
there was plenty of green chalk …

then added foliage and
a palm tree as big as a dandelion.

The Twins (still ruffled over
their smudged flowers)
added a cloud,

and Cecilia
an alien invader.

Arthur's bird of paradise
sat in the palm tree.

Rosie stood in the cloud.

She pondered.

She thought.

Here is what she made.

The Queen of Swirls

Someone drew butterflies
and balloons, a caterpillar,
and a bumblebee passing by.

A beautiful and exotic garden
spread across the concrete.
And the Queen of Swirls ruled.

Nasrin, lonely for her mum in
faraway Isfahan, took a picture…

"I'm missing you, Mum. A concrete garden –
isn't it something?" And she pressed SEND.

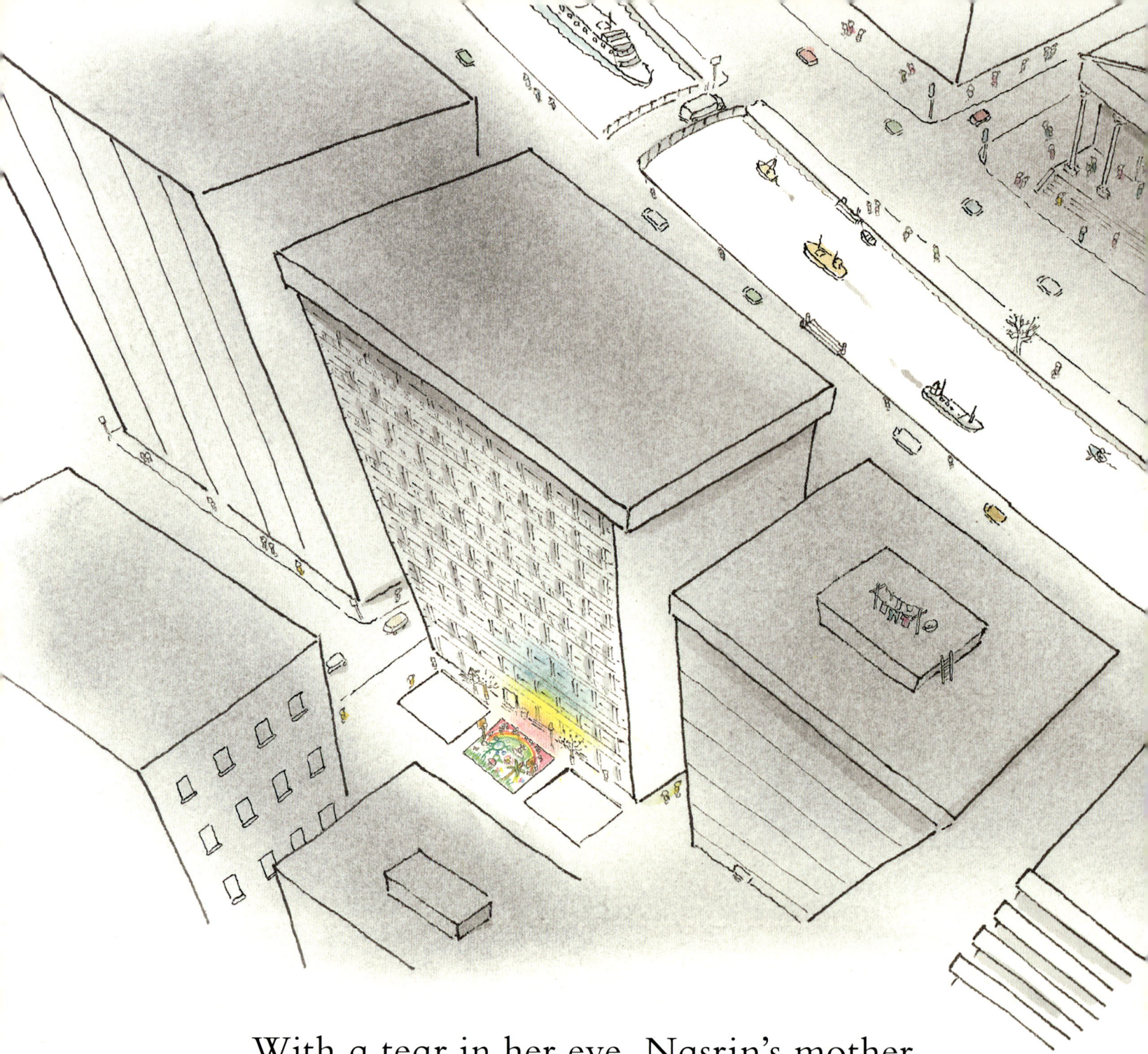

With a tear in her eye, Nasrin's mother
then sent it on to everyone she knew.
The picture crossed deserts
and mountains and oceans and cities.

It bounced across the world, returning
to fill the screens in all the dark rooms
over the concrete garden.

The people
came outside
and applauded.

The Queen of Swing

And the children took a bow!

Someone threw flowers.

For three whole days
the Queen of Swirls
ruled over the garden.

On the fourth, it rained.
It washed the chalk
garden clean away!

And the rain stopped.

Not in the least bit sad,
the children once more
burst from the building.

Amanda was last again,
and with no chalks left …

she ripped her empty box.

The kids raced
their cardboard boats.

And the concrete garden's gutters
ran with rainbows.

Amanda gave the box
remains to her mum.

DING!

The lift arrived and
they returned
to the fifteenth floor.